ABDO Publishing Company is the exclusive school and library distributor of Rabbit Ears Books.

Library bound edition 2005.

Library of Congress Cataloging-in-Publication Data

Kessler, Brad.
  Brer Rabbit and Boss Lion / collected by Joel Chandler Harris ; written by Brad Kessler ;
illustrated by Bill Mayer.
        p. cm.
  "Rabbit Ears books."
  Summary: Boss Lion threatens to eat all the inhabitants of the village, until he is
outsmarted by Brer Rabbit.
  ISBN 1-59197-760-6
  [1. African Americans—Folklore. 2. Animals—Folklore. 3. Folklore—United States.] I.
Harris, Joel, Chandler, 1848-1908. II. Mayer, Bill, ill. III. Title.

PZ8.1.K48Br 2004
398.2—dc22
[E]

                                                                            2004047729

All Rabbit Ears books are reinforced library binding
and manufactured in the United States of America.

BRER RABBIT

and Boss Lion

· · · · · · · · · · · · · · · ·

Collected by Joel Chandler Harris

Written by Brad Kessler

Illustrated by Bill Mayer

RABBIT EARS BOOKS

ay down in the deepest South, along the river they now call the Mississippi, there once lived an assembly of animals who were all the best of friends. Now this was a good long time ago. So long ago that most folks forget—but some still remember—how the animals in Brer Village got along just as kindly as any a critter could. They helped each other out of fixes and fixed each other out of hard times. Things were peaceable and pleasant, generally speaking that is.

But one day all that changed when Boss Lion, the king of the forest as he liked to call himself, came along and set himself down in an old cave on the outskirts of Brer Village.

Now, as everyone knows, or ought to know, Boss Lion was not a fella to be messing with. He was the meanest, baddest, biggest, smelliest, proudest, fattest cat in the forest—and he was not so nice besides. He had a mouthful of scissor-sharp teeth. He had claws that could cut clear through a cottonwood tree, and a mane of hair that he kept slicked and oiled at all times. And this here Boss Lion—if it isn't clear already—was certainly no vegetarian.

And sure as a hog's a pig and vice versa, Boss Lion lived up to his ferocious reputation. He gobbled up pawsful of gooselings. He swallowed a six-pack of piglets. He lay about on the outskirts of town, fat and mean, doing not a lick of work, eating up whatever animal came along, and being just generally antisocial in his behavior.

After a few days, them Brer folks had enough of Boss Lion and held a meeting to see what they could do about him.

They gathered in the center of town and argued back and forth, this way and that, then that way and this, and a few other ways besides. And finally they decided that someone would have to go to Boss Lion and explain to him the score: If he kept up the way he was doing, he would destroy the village and there wouldn't be any more animals left to live there.

Things were getting so bad, they decided to make a deal with Boss Lion: If he promised to stay inside his cave, they would come every day to feed him.

Then Brer Fox stepped forward and cleared his throat.

"Well, folks," he said, "seein' that we've got that matter settled, all we've got to do now is figure out who's gonna talk to Boss Lion."

At that, all them folks fell suddenly silent. After a couple of minutes, Brer Pig snorted and spoke up.

"I wouldn't mind one bit tellin' that ole lion what we've decided here, but I've got some rootin' to do before the rains come." And then Brer Bear came forward.

"I'd love to give Boss Lion a piece of my mind," he said, "but I'm behind on my berry

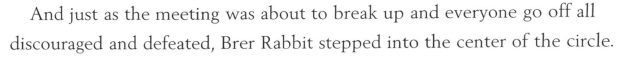

And just as the meeting was about to break up and everyone go off all discouraged and defeated, Brer Rabbit stepped into the center of the circle.

"I swear by my white whiskers," he said, "ya'll might be too tender-footed to tell that mangy-hide lion what we think of him, but I'm not!"

harvest, and I've got to make fruit cocktail for the cubs."

Then everyone started talking all at once. Brer Coon said he had to get his hay in from the field. Brer Goose said he had to take care of his wife while she laid an egg. Brer Gobble had a headache and needed to buy some aspirin, and Brer Frog had to get a haircut and then needed to paint his pad. It looked as if no one was going to talk to Boss Lion.

Now Brer Rabbit was not a very big fella. Fact, even as hares go, he was a puny sort of guy, always getting himself into all kinds of unaccountable trouble on account of that big mouth of his.

So Brer Gobble shouted out: "Brer Rabbit, you can't go to Boss Lion. He's ten times bigger than you!"

"Yeah," Brer Fox added, chuckling to himself, "that lion will eat you up as an appetizer and make a key chain out of your foot."

"Now listen, folks," Brer Rabbit said, "I'm gonna tell you now—and y'all listen good. Brer Rabbit ain't afraid of nobody, certainly not some scurvy-breathed, greasy-headed, flea-infested, boil-faced Boss Lion. Appetizer! I'm off right now to pulverize his paw, kick him in the jaw, and maybe even mispronounce his name if I feel like it. We'll see who makes a key chain out of who!"

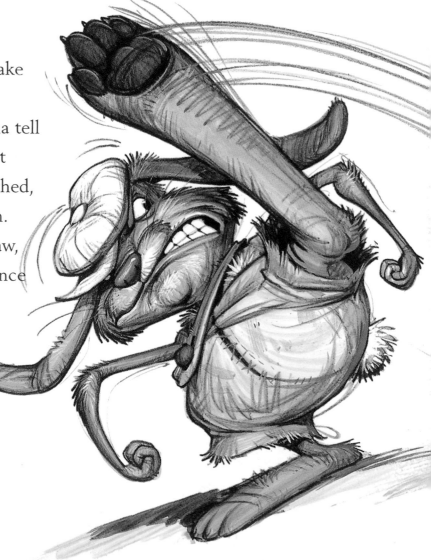

And with that, Brer Rabbit hitched up his pants and pulled his duck-cloth cap over one eye. He removed a cigar from his breast pocket, put it in his mouth, and sauntered off to the outskirts of the village, whistling the entire time as if he were heading to the fish hole to hook him a bullheaded catfish.

Yet the minute Brer Rabbit turned a corner and was out of view from the rest of the villagers, he stopped whistling and stubbed out his cigar. He fixed his cap straight on his head, and the closer he came to Boss Lion's cave, the more he started sweating and shaking, until his legs were wobbling so bad he could hardly walk straight.

When he got to Boss Lion's cave, he took his cap off and knocked meekly on the door.

The door flew open and Boss Lion stood in the threshold breathing straight down Brer Rabbit's neck.

"Who are you and what do you want?"

"Umm, uhhh, ahh . . . it's me, Brer Rabbit," he stuttered.

"What do you want?" Boss Lion demanded again.

"Uhh, the folks here had a little meeting and they asked me to tell you, since you are the big boss, it's not right that you should have to get your own food. They says that if you'd stay at home all the time they'd be just plumb honored to bring you all the food you'd ever want."

"I want fresh meat three times a day!" Boss Lion growled at Brer Rabbit. His breath was something awful. "And if they don't bring it to me, I'll eat them all up and destroy their village!"

"Yes, sir . . . yes, sir, Mr. Boss Lion," Brer Rabbit stammered. "They will bring you meat three times a day, sir, and good eatin' meat at that, sir. You can count on me 'cause I'll make sure of it personally." With that, Brer Rabbit lit off like buckshot, as fast as his furry feet could take him.

But as soon as Brer Rabbit drew near the village, he stopped to catch his breath. He fished out his old cigar, cocked his cap back over one eye, and ambled into town, just as calmly as if he were on his way back from the fish hole.

When they saw him coming they all ran out to greet him. "Did you see Boss Lion?" they asked. "What did he say? Did he eat you up as an appetizer? Were you scared?"

Brer Rabbit silenced them with a wave of his paw.

"Lord Almighty, I've told you time and again that Brer Rabbit ain't afraid of no fat cat lion. You asked me to tell him your mind, and I did."

Those folks were considerably curious, and demanded of Brer Rabbit a full accounting of what had happened.

"Well," he said, "I went straight up to that cave, invited myself in, and sat down on a chair across from Boss Lion. And I put it to him directly, sayin': 'Look here, Mr. Lion, you're disturbin' the peace of our village, not to say eatin' us all alive. Now none of us folks like to see another starve, so we'll feed you ourselves. But you've got to stay in your cave at all times, and got to eat whatever we give you, otherwise I'll personally kick the livin' kidneys out of you and lock you up in the hoosegow!'

"Well, that old cat growled and barked a bit, but he saw I meant some serious business, and that I wasn't scared of him one whit. So he turned it over a piece and then agreed.

But one thing," Brer Rabbit added. "We got to feed him three times a day."

At this, a big roar of praise rose up from the crowd and everyone talked about how brave Brer Rabbit was. But after a minute, the hubbub died down, and a few folks started wondering aloud where the meat would come from, and who was going to feed Boss Lion first.

Well, wouldn't you know it, they all started yammering and quarreling and pointing and screaming at each other.

"You first! You first!"

So Brer Rabbit held up his paw again and suggested they draw straws. Brer Rabbit just happened to have a few straws in his back pocket. So he held them in his fist and all the folks drew straws.

Now it came to pass that Brer Goose picked the short one. And when he saw it, he hemmed and hawed and honked out loud, "Nope, nope, nope!"

And Brer Rabbit said, "Yup, yup, yup!" and pointed in the direction of Boss Lion's cave on the outskirts of town.

So Brer Goose hung his beak low and headed out to Boss Lion's cave, stopping at home first to cook an omelette for Boss Lion. And when he got to Boss Lion's cave, it was just about twilight, which is to say suppertime.

Boss Lion gobbled up Brer Goose, and ate the omelette for dessert.

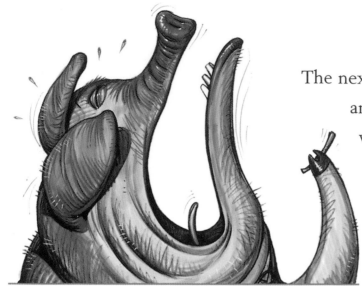

The next morning, Brer Rabbit held the straws again, and this time Brer Pig drew the short one. And when he saw it he squealed and screamed and oinked out loud, "Nope, nope, nope!"

And Brer Rabbit said, "Yup, yup, yup!" and pointed in the direction of Boss Lion's cave on the outskirts of town. So Brer Pig hung his head low and made his way to Boss Lion's cave, stopping first at home to get a milk shake for Boss Lion. And when he got to Boss Lion's cave, it was breakfast time, and Boss Lion ate Brer Pig right up, and used the milk shake to shampoo his hair.

And so it went on like this at each feeding time for a couple of days, with Brer folks going out to feed Boss Lion and never coming back again.

And on the third day, at lunchtime, Brer
Fox up and made an announcement:
"It's my turn now to hold the straws."

He peered over at Brer Rabbit, and a thin smile of satisfaction spread across his face.

He had been watching Brer Rabbit and realized that as long as Brer Rabbit held the straws, he would send everybody else to feed Boss Lion except himself. So when Brer Fox held the straws that afternoon, sure enough, Brer Rabbit picked the short one.

When Brer Rabbit saw his straw, he didn't hem or haw or honk. Instead he grew pale and pensive, and said out loud to no one in particular:

"Well if that ain't the cat's tail itself. I'm a pickled bunny in a barrel."

And then he hopped up on an old tree stump, cleared his throat, and addressed his fellow critters.

"Critters," he said, "we sure had some good times together, some laughs, some cries, some close calls. But now it looks like my time is up and I suppose I'm aimin' to be an appetizer for that old lion. So pray for me, folks, and perhaps soon we'll all meet in that big fish hole in the sky. Good-bye ladies. Good-bye gentlemen—and good-bye Brer Fox."

And he hung his head mighty low and walked out of the village into the leafy cool of the afternoon. And all those folks were so moved that tears began rolling down their faces.

Now Brer Rabbit was in no considerable rush to get to Boss Lion's cave. So he decided to make a detour and see his farm for the very last time. He took

off through the woods and when he arrived there, he looked over his carrot patch.

"Good-bye carrot patch," he said, waving to the green shoots of carrots in the ground. He saw his shovel and said good-bye to it. "I'm shoving off myself, Mr. Shovel. Nice to have worked with you."

Then he walked to his well to bid it good-bye and take a last drink of sweet water.

"Farewell, trusty well," he said, and he saw his reflection in the bottom of the well. And when he saw his reflection, he got such a good idea that he yelled out loud: "Yes sir! You are a fair well, because you're always lookin' out for my welfare!"

And at that he scampered off, tippity-top, like the wind itself, to Boss Lion's cave.

By the time he got to the cave, it was getting on toward evening. The sun was setting behind the cottonwoods, and the evening swallows were in the air. Lunch had long passed, and Boss Lion was mighty angry at that.

"Where is my meat, rabbit? You are late with my meat!"

"I tried to get here as soon as I could—it's the Lord's truth. You see, I had so much meat for you that I couldn't carry it all by myself, so I stashed it away. And if you'll follow me, I can take you to it."

Boss Lion looked as if he were about to pounce on Brer Rabbit and gobble him up right there, so Brer Rabbit had to do some mighty lickety-split fast-fire talking.

"Look here Boss Lion," he pleaded. "I'm just a teeny rabbit and I'd only be an appetizer to a big lion like you. Why, I wouldn't even be an appetizer, I'd be just a bite of fur and bones. You couldn't even put me on a cracker, I'm so small. But if you want a whole locker of meat, a great big pile of fresh juicy steaks, I promise I'll show you. I promise."

"Take me
to the meat!
And it better
be enough or
I'll eat you right
now!"

And so they took off together through the woods to Brer Rabbit's farm.

When they reached his well, Brer Rabbit opened the door, looked in, and fell backwards, as if he had been stung by a honeybee.

"Lord Almighty!" he yelled to Boss Lion. "There's some big critter in there and he's eatin' your meat!"

Boss Lion pushed Brer Rabbit aside and stuck his head in the well. "Who are you?" he growled down into the deep well.

And a few seconds later his echo came back up, "Who are you-u-u?"

Now old Boss Lion was not used to being talked back to, seeing as he was the king of the forest and all. And when he heard the voice boiling back up from the well, he grew awfully angry and roared back down. "Who am I? I says, who are you?"

And once again, the voice came back: "Who am I? I says, who-o-o-o are you-u-u-u?"

Boss Lion was now turning strawberry-red with rage, huffing and snorting and growling. And just then Brer Rabbit poked him in the side.

"You hear him sass you?" he said. "That lion down there is eatin' your meat and makin' a mockery out of you. You gonna take that from him? Why, curse his pile-of-fresh-meat-stealin' soul! I'll whup that lion down there myself if he has the guts to get up here."

Boss Lion looked into the well again, and saw a lion staring right back up at him—a mean and ugly lion. And he yelled at him, "I'm gonna get you!"

He yelled directly back at Boss Lion, "I'm gonna get you!" And this was just about all Boss Lion could handle.

"Step back, rabbit! That cat's dead meat!" And with that, Boss Lion took a flying leap right into that well.

There was a great crash deep inside—*ker-plunge!*—and as soon as Brer Rabbit heard it, he slammed the lid shut and locked it.

After a few seconds of silence, he took out his cap, cocked it on his head, and pulled out his old cigar.

And he sauntered off into town at a leisurely pace while the last streaks of sunlight were softening over the forest.

When he got near the village, all the folks were standing around debating who was going to feed Boss Lion next. And when they saw Brer Rabbit coming down the road in the gloam, they thought for sure he was a ghost, and started running to save their souls. But Brer Rabbit stopped them and told them he was no ghost, and as soon as they realized it was so, they asked him, all excitedly, "Didn't Boss Lion eat you up?"

"Eat who up?" Brer Rabbit asked back. "Me? No, ain't no confounded lion come near to these naps of mine."

"What did he say?" the folks asked. "What did he do? Won't he come to eat us all up now?"

And at that, Brer Rabbit laughed and explained to them what he had done. Well, he changed the story around a little and said that when Boss Lion started getting rough with him, he simply beat the living kidneys out of him, as he had promised he would, and threw him into the well.

And though most folks didn't believe him at first, he later showed them the well, and the drowned troublemaker at the bottom, so they had to believe him.

And for many, many years afterwards, Brer Rabbit was a hero in those parts along the Mississippi River. People told stories about him and sang his praises for acres around. And things were pretty peaceable once more in Brer

Village, except for a few small scrapes here and there, and maybe a minor spat now and then. But as long as anyone can remember, no Boss Lions ever came by again to bother the folks of Brer Village.

The  End